P9-CJM-390

Glad or Sad-- How Do You Feel?

by the editors of
The Child's World

illustrated by
Frances Hook

ELGIN, ILLINOIS 60120

Library of Congress Cataloging in Publication Data

Child's World (Firm)
Glad or sad, how do you feel?

Edition of 1973 published under title: How do you feel?
SUMMARY: Explores a child's feelings in various situations and the feelings God has for us.
1. Emotions—Juvenile literature. [1. Emotions. 2. Christian life] I. Hook, Frances. II. Title.
BF561.C54 1979 152.4′4 79-12152
ISBN 0-89565-072-X

Distributed by Standard Publishing, 8121 Hamilton Avenue, Cincinnati, Ohio 45231.

Glad or Sad-- How Do You Feel?

"Be glad in the Lord. . .
and shout for joy."

—PSALM 32:11.

"God is our refuge and strength,
a very present help in trouble."

—PSALM 46:1.

How do you feel when
you want something
very, very much?

How do you feel when
you get it for your
birthday?

You feel happy
because you know
someone cares for you.

God cares for you too.
He gave you
the gift of Life.

HAPPY
BIRTHDAY

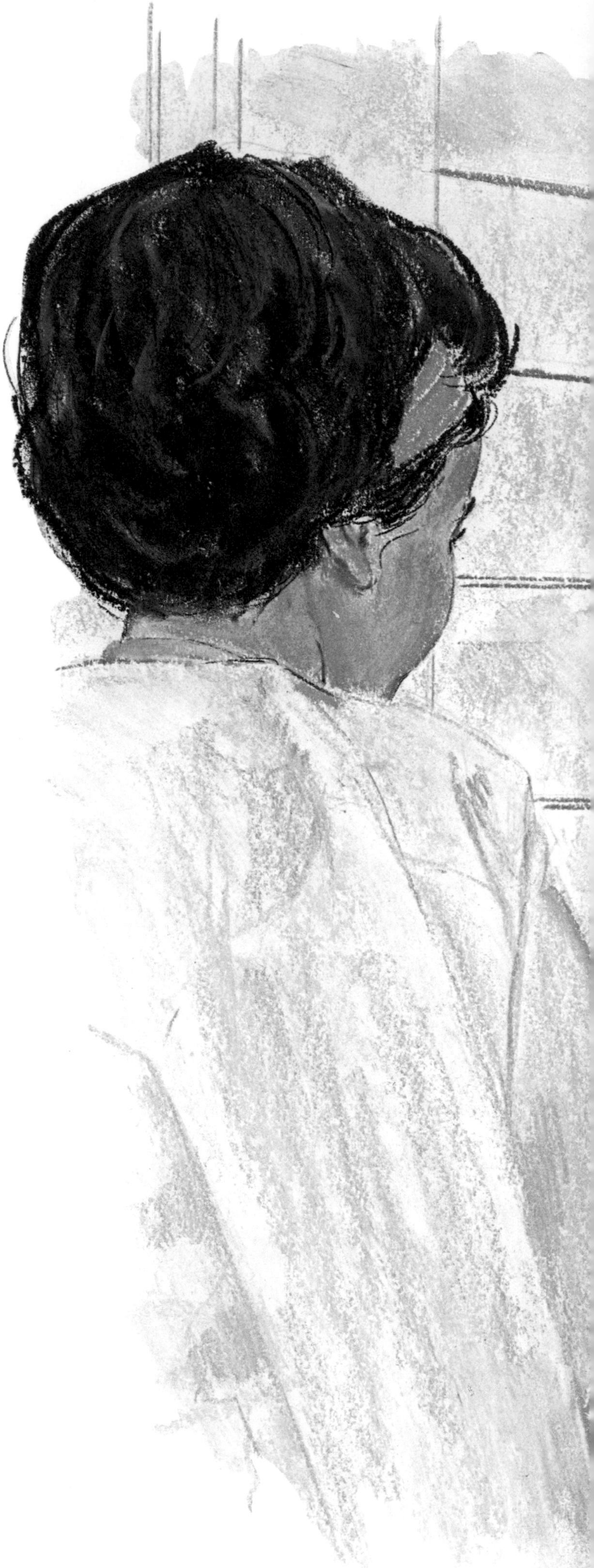

How do you
feel when Mother
leaves you
for a little while?

Sometimes Mother
has a job to do
and has to go
away. But even though
she leaves you...

Y Hook

she comes back,
and you feel her love
when you are in her arms.

God loves you too.

How do you feel when
your pet is hurt?

L.HOOK

How do you feel when
your pet is better?

You feel happy because
you love your pet
so much.

Your Heavenly Father
loves you even more,
because you are His child.

How do you feel when
someone hurts you?

How do you feel when
someone helps you?

God helps you in many ways.
Do you help others?

How do you feel when
you are all alone?

How do you feel when
friends come to play?

Jesus is your friend too.
He is your best friend.

How do you feel when
you can't get your boots on?

How do you feel when
you ask for help and someone
helps you put them on?

God is a Helper too.
When you ask God to guide you
in His way of love and kindness,
He will.

Sometimes we forget
God's way.
We fuss and fight.
We hurt each other.

Then we remember God's way.
We say, "I'm sorry."
We forgive each other
and make things right again.

When you make things right
with a friend,
how do you feel?